There's something spooky going on in the concert ticket line.

"Someone should stop that ghost," Eric said. "He's scaring lots of people."

The ghost yelled, "Boo!" and waved his arms at a group of teenagers. They yelled, "Boo!" and waved their arms back at him.

Then the ghost held up his arms and ran in circles around a small boy and his mother. When the ghost yelled, "Boo!" the boy grabbed onto his mother and cried.

"Scaring young children is not funny," Aunt Molly said.

"That's an evil ghost," the man in the suit said.

"Hey, you!" a security guard from the back of the line called out. "Stop that!"

CASE #16

The Ghostly Mystery

David A. Adler

Illustrated by Susanna Natti

PUFFIN BOOKS
An Imprint of Penguin Group (USA) Inc.

PUFFIN BOOKS

Published by the Penguin Group

Penguin Young Readers Group, 345 Hudson Street, New York, New York 10014, U.S.A.

Penguin Group (Canada), 90 Eglinton Avenue East, Suite 700, Toronto, Ontario, Canada M4P 2Y3
(a division of Pearson Penguin Canada Inc.)

Penguin Books Ltd, 80 Strand, London WC2R 0RL, England

Penguin Ireland, 25 St Stephen's Green, Dublin 2, Ireland (a division of Penguin Books Ltd)

Penguin Group (Australia), 250 Camberwell Road, Camberwell, Victoria 3124, Australia
(a division of Pearson Australia Group Pty Ltd)

Penguin Books India Pvt Ltd, 11 Community Centre,
Panchsheel Park, New Delhi - 110 017, India

Penguin Group (NZ), 67 Apollo Drive, Rosedale, North Shore 0632, New Zealand
(a division of Pearson New Zealand Ltd)

Penguin Books (South Africa) (Pty) Ltd, 24 Sturdee Avenue,
Rosebank, Johannesburg 2196, South Africa

Registered Offices: Penguin Books Ltd, 80 Strand, London WC2R 0RL, England

First published in the United States of America by Viking,
a division of Penguin Books USA Inc., 1996

Published by Puffin Books, a division of Penguin Young Readers Group, 1998, 2005

This edition published by Puffin Books, a division of Penguin Young Readers Group, 2011

15 17 19 20 18 16

THE LIBRARY OF CONGRESS HAS CATALOGED THE VIKING EDITION AS FOLLOWS:
Adler, David A.
Cam Jansen and the ghostly mystery / David A. Adler ; illustrated by Susanna Natti.
p. cm.—(A Cam Jansen adventure ; 16)
Summary: Cam uses her photographic memory to catch a thief disguised as a ghost.
ISBN: 0-670-86872-8 (hardcover)
[1. Robbers and outlaws—Fiction . 2. Ghosts—Fiction. 3. Mystery and detective stories.]
I. Natti, Susanna, ill. II. Title. III. Series: Adler, David A. Cam Jansen adventure ; 16.
PZ7.A2615Caaf 1996
[Fic]—dc20
96-15250 CIP AC

Puffin Books ISBN 978-0-14-240287-0

Printed in the United States of America

For Alyse,
Samuel,
Hillel,
and Jacob

Chapter One

"Look at him," Cam Jansen said. She pointed to someone wearing a costume with three horns. "He looks like a triceratops."

Eric pointed to someone else and said, "And look at her. She looks like Tyrannosaurus rex."

Cam Jansen, her friend Eric Shelton, and Cam's aunt Molly were waiting in line. They wanted to buy tickets to a Triceratops Pops concert. Triceratops Pops is a singing group. They wear dinosaur costumes when they perform. Sometimes their fans wear costumes, too.

"I went to a concert in London," Aunt Molly said. "Someone there was dressed in a piano and he played a tuxedo."

Cam looked at Eric. Then they both looked at Aunt Molly.

Aunt Molly laughed. "Oh, my. I said that wrong. The man was dressed in a tuxedo and he played a piano."

Aunt Molly thought a moment. "And it wasn't in London. It was in Paris."

Cam stepped out of line. She looked at all the people ahead of her. They were all waiting to buy tickets.

"I hope there are still tickets left for us," Cam said.

The man standing behind Cam smiled and asked, "Excuse me, but isn't this a long line for a science talk?"

The man was wearing a dark suit and tie. He was carrying a large leather briefcase.

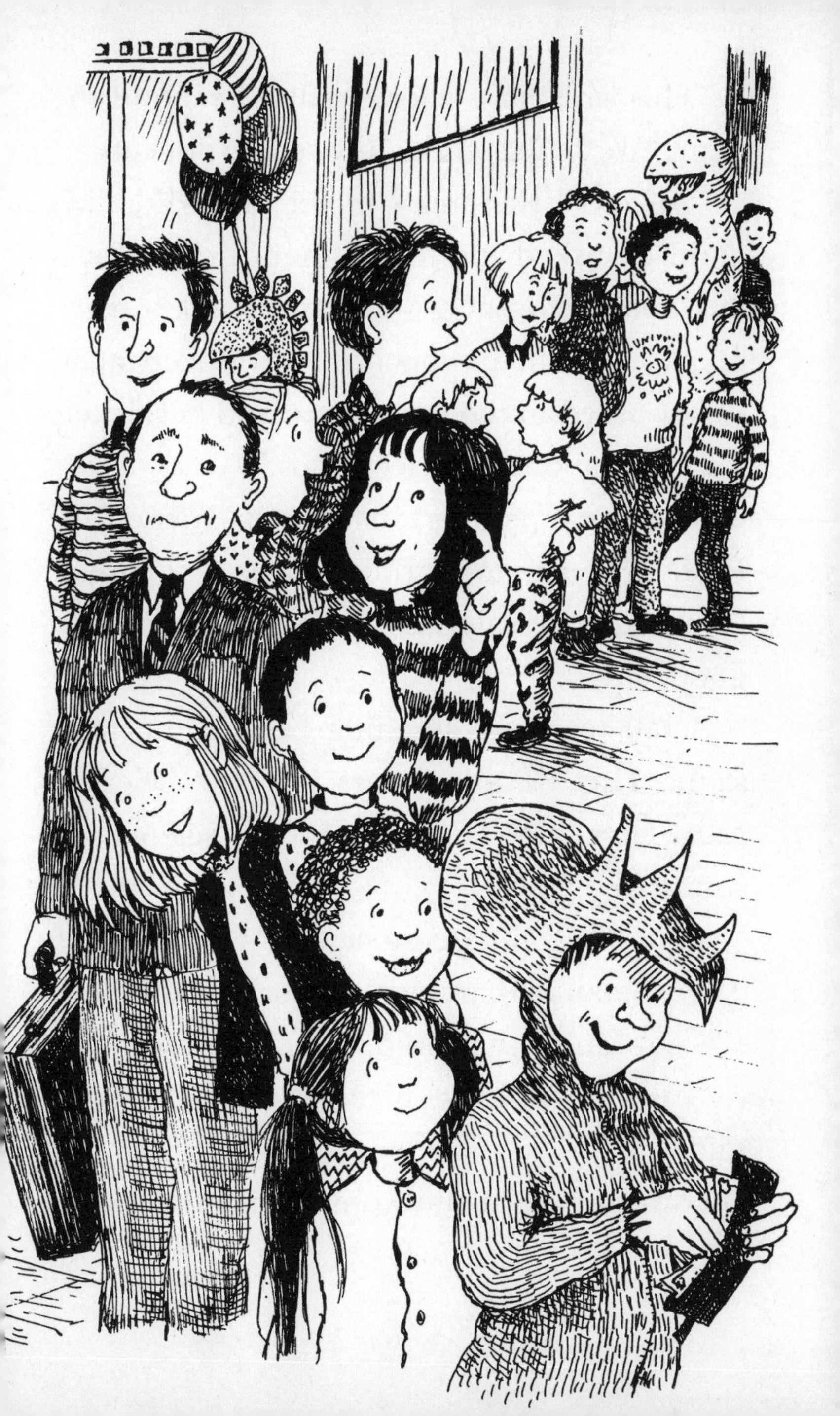

"This isn't for a science talk," Eric told the man. "We're waiting to buy concert tickets."

"Oh, no," the man in the suit said. "My children asked me to get them tickets for a talk about dinosaurs." The man took a piece of paper from his pocket and looked at it. "They asked me to come here and get tickets for a talk about the triceratops."

"This is a concert hall, and Triceratops Pops is a singing group," Eric explained. "Some people call them T-Pops. They're very good."

A tall teenager standing behind the man said, "The T-Pops singers are into science, too. They are masters of the 'science of sound.'"

Aunt Molly pointed to a woman walking by. The woman had green and purple hair.

Aunt Molly whispered, "She looks strange."

"I think she looks nice," the tall teenager said.

Cam looked at the woman with the green

4

and purple hair. Cam blinked her eyes and said, "*Click*. She looks interesting. I want to remember her."

Cam Jansen has a photographic memory. It's as if she has a mental camera and there are photographs in her head of everything

she has seen. Cam says *"Click"* is the sound her mental camera makes when it takes a picture.

Cam's real name is Jennifer Jansen. But when people found out about her mental camera, they began calling her "The Camera." Soon "The Camera" was shortened to "Cam."

Cam closed her eyes. She said, *"Click,"* again.

"We've seen lots of interesting people in the city," Cam said, with her eyes still closed. "Right now I'm looking at a picture I have in my head of a man Eric and I saw. The man was carrying lots of signs. He even had words painted on his clothing."

"I remember one of the signs," Eric said. "'Air is free! Water is free! Food should be free, too!'"

Cam said, *"Click,"* again.

"Now I'm looking at a picture I have in my head of the Bell Woman."

"She had bell earrings," Eric told Aunt Molly, "and bells on her necklace and her bracelet, too. When she walked, she jingled."

Just then a ghost jumped in front of Aunt Molly.

"Eek!" Aunt Molly screamed. "Oh, my!"

Chapter Two

Cam opened her eyes.

Someone wearing a ghost costume was standing in front of Aunt Molly. The "ghost" was wearing a large white sheet, black gloves, and a scary gray mask. He waved his arms and shouted, "Boo!"

Cam looked at the ghost, blinked her eyes, and said, *"Click."*

Aunt Molly put her hand to her heart. She held on to Eric and said, "Oh, my."

Eric whispered, "It's not a real ghost."

Eric pointed and said, "He's wearing sneakers. Real ghosts don't wear sneakers."

The ghost waved his arms and shouted, "Boo!" again. Then he jumped in front of someone else.

"What a curious thing to do," the man in the suit said. "This dinosaur singing group seems to attract odd fans."

"Excuse me," Cam said, "but I'm not odd."

"Someone should stop that ghost," Eric said. "He's scaring lots of people."

The ghost yelled, "Boo!" and waved his arms at a group of teenagers. They yelled, "Boo!" and waved their arms back at him.

Then the ghost held up his arms and ran in circles around a small boy and his mother. When the ghost yelled, "Boo!" the boy grabbed onto his mother and cried.

"Scaring young children is not funny," Aunt Molly said.

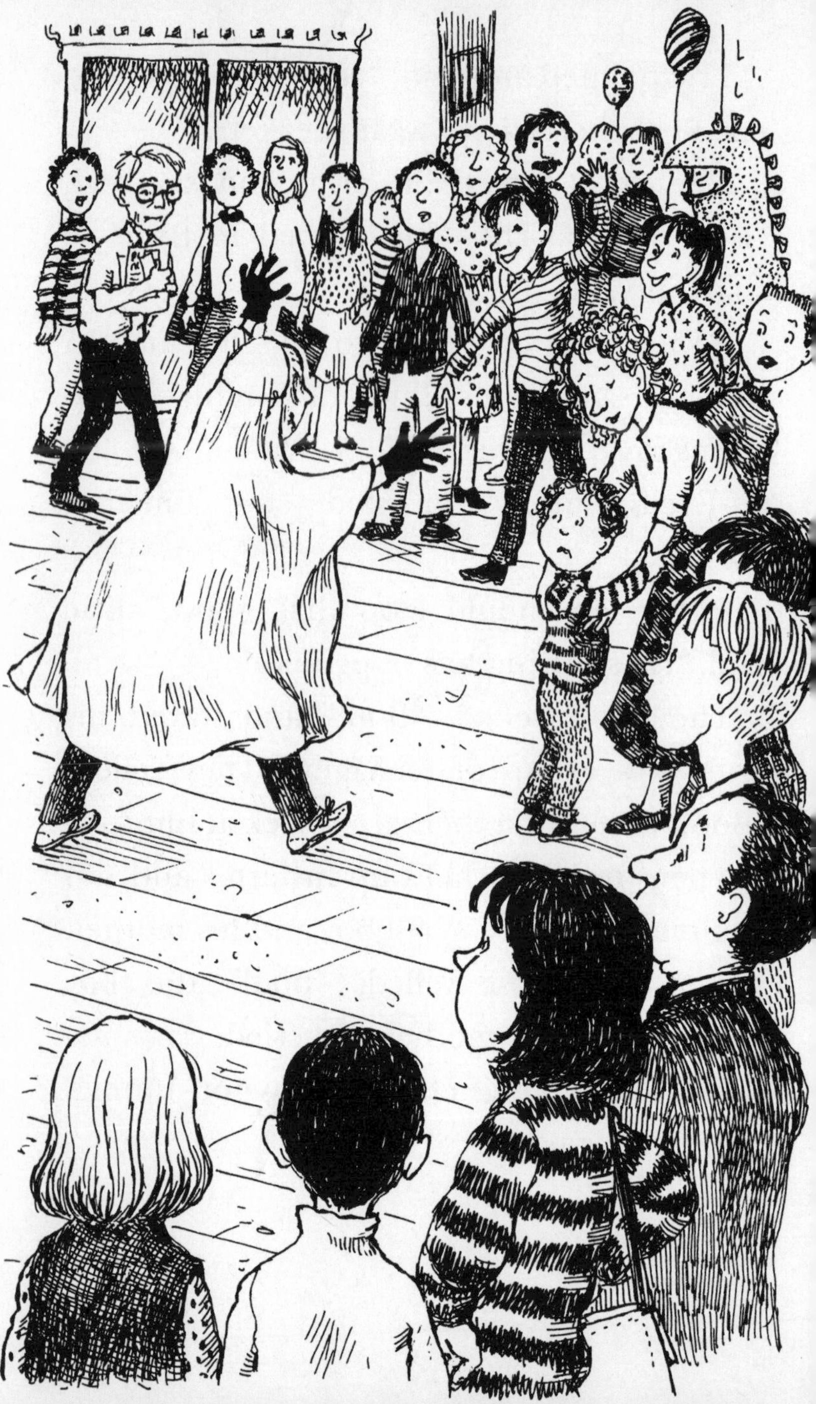

"That's an evil ghost," the man in the suit said.

"Hey, you!" a security guard from the back of the line called out. "Stop that!"

The guard was hurrying toward the ghost.

Another guard was running from the front of the line.

They chased the ghost away from the line and into the train station. The entrance to the station was just past the end of the line.

Lots of people were leaving the train station. They hurried past the ghost. Some smiled when they saw his costume.

The ghost walked up to a short old man wearing a bright yellow shirt. The man was bent slightly forward. He was holding papers and magazines to his chest. He didn't seem to notice the ghost.

"Oh, no!" Aunt Molly said. "I hope he doesn't scare that old man."

But that's just what the ghost did.

The ghost jumped in front of him. The ghost waved his arms and yelled, "Boo!"

The old man looked up and saw the ghost. The old man opened his mouth as if he was about to scream. But he didn't. His hands fell to his sides. His papers and magazines scattered. The man clutched his heart and dropped to the ground.

Chapter Three

The old man's arms and legs were stretched out. His glasses had fallen off. His newspapers and magazines were on the ground.

The guards and a few people from the line ran to the man. A teenaged girl was the first to get to him. She shook the man and said, "Get up! Get up!"

The man didn't move.

"I knew it!" Aunt Molly said. "He was so scared that he had a heart attack."

The ghost turned. He looked at the guards and the people. Then he ran off.

One of the guards and two teenagers chased after the ghost. But then the old man opened his eyes.

He moaned. "Oh! Oh! Help!"

The guard and the teenagers turned. They ran to the man.

The old man put his hand to his heart. He closed his eyes.

"I'll call for an ambulance," one guard told the other. "You stay here."

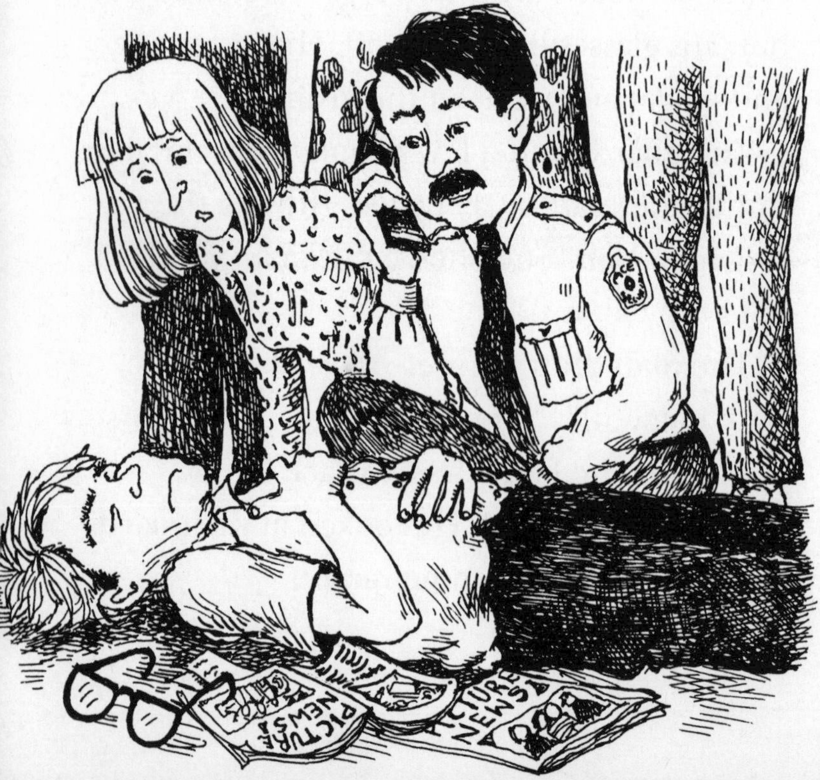
PICTURE NEWS

The guard took a small telephone from his pocket. He spoke into it. He said there was an emergency. He spoke about the old man and gave his location.

"Step back," the other guard said. "Give him air."

"Just a minute," the guard talking into the telephone said. He hurried to the old man. He bent close to the man's face and listened.

Cam whispered to Eric, "He's checking if the man is breathing."

Then the guard picked up the man's hand.

"Now he's checking the man's pulse," Cam said.

The guard spoke into the telephone again.

"He's breathing. His pulse is steady."

The guard held the telephone close to his ear for another minute and listened. Then he put the telephone in his pocket.

The other guard called out, "Is there a doctor here?"

"I'm a baker," someone said.

"I'm a teacher."

"I run a large business," the man in the suit said. "We sell cloth to stores all over the world."

"This man needs a doctor, not someone who sells cloth," the guard said.

"My cousin is a doctor," one woman said, "and I know what to do. Raise the man's head."

"No. Raise his feet," someone else said.

"Breathe into his mouth."

"No. Just leave him alone."

The guard looked at the old man. The old man took a deep breath. He opened his eyes. He looked at the guard and the crowd. He took another deep breath and closed his eyes again.

"Look," Cam whispered. She pointed at the old man's hair. "He's wearing a wig. When he fell his hair moved. He has brown hair under a white wig."

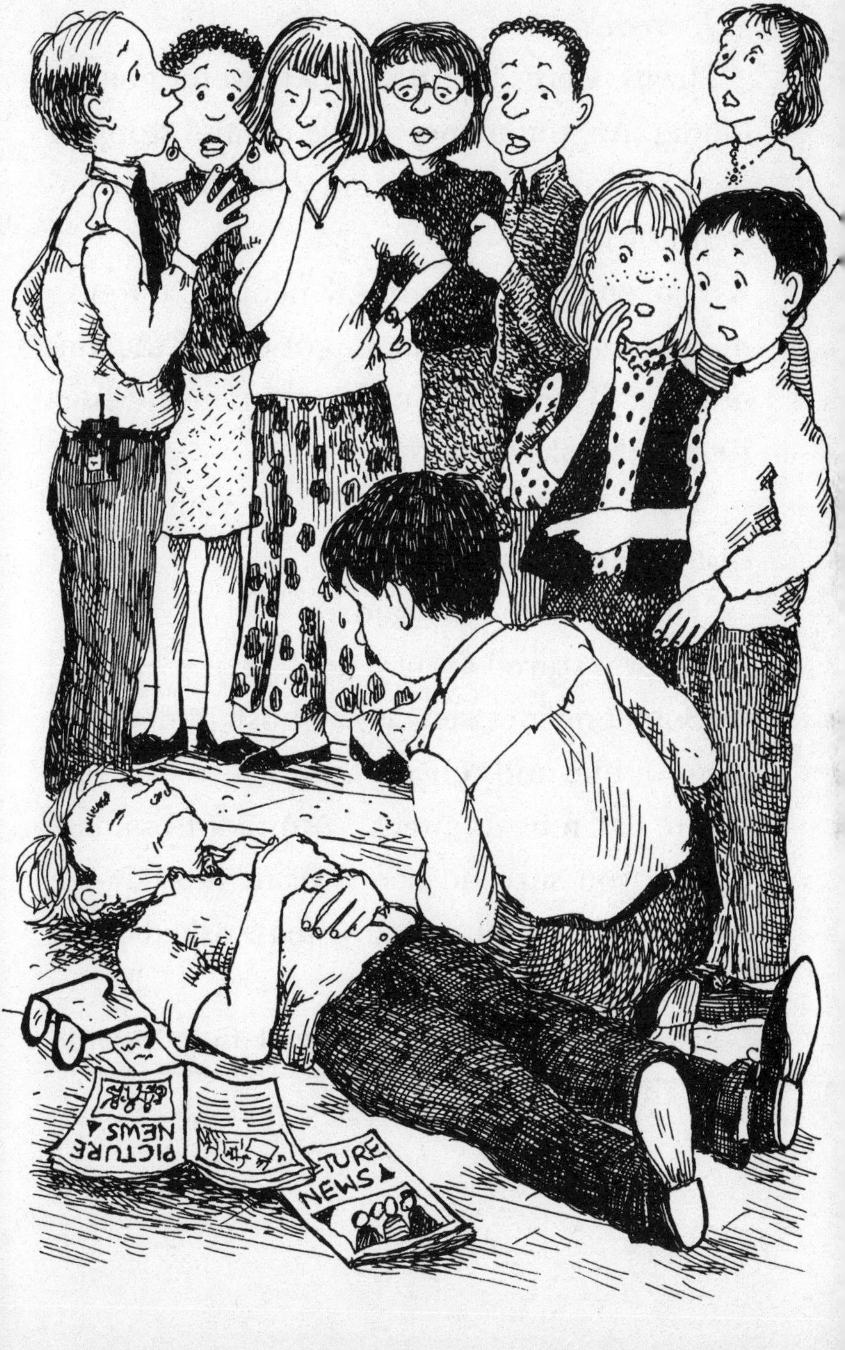
PICTURE NEWS
TURE NEWS

Rrrrrrr!

Sirens were blaring. They were getting louder. An ambulance drove up and stopped near where Cam, Eric, and Aunt Molly were standing.

Two emergency medical people, a young man and a young woman, got out of the ambulance. They took out a stretcher and hurried to the old man.

"What happened here?" the young man from the ambulance asked.

"He fell," someone said.

"He was scared and he fell."

"Someone dressed as a ghost jumped in front of him and yelled, 'Boo!'"

"He had a heart attack," Aunt Molly said.

"Are you sure he had a heart attack? Are you a doctor?" the young man asked Aunt Molly.

"No. I work for an airline. I help people plan their vacations."

The young man told his partner, "He may have just fainted. But we should take him to the emergency room for a full checkup."

The old man opened his eyes and looked at the stretcher and ambulance. Then he spoke very softly.

"What did you say?" the young woman asked.

She told everyone to be quiet. Then she bent close to the old man.

The old man spoke again.

"I still can't hear you," the young woman said. "Could you speak louder?"

Suddenly someone shouted, "Help! Help! I've been robbed!"

Chapter Four

The shouts came from the front of the line.

Cam turned. Eric and the others standing around the old man turned, too.

"I've been robbed! I've been robbed!" a woman said as she walked quickly toward the two guards.

The guards walked to the woman. They knew her.

"Sally, what happened?" one of the guards asked.

"I was sitting in the ticket booth," Sally said. "And someone pointed a gun at me."

Sally wiped a tear from her cheek. "It was awful," she said.

"What happened next?" a guard asked.

Sally took a deep breath and said, "He waved the gun and said, 'Give me all the money.'"

Sally wiped away another tear.

"So I gave him everything in the cash box. I sold a lot of tickets this morning. I know there was a lot of money in that box.

"'Now give me *your* money,' he said.

"My purse was by the desk. I emptied it. He took my lunch money. He took the money for the train ride home. He took everything."

One guard took the telephone from his pocket. He called the police and told them that there had been a robbery.

The other guard asked Sally, "Can you describe the thief?"

"He was about my height," Sally said. "And he was wearing sneakers. I know that. But I never saw his face. He was wearing a ghost costume."

"That ghost scared that poor old man, too," someone said.

The old man was standing up now. He was listening to Sally.

"And he scared my child," a woman said.

The guards walked with Sally to the ticket booth. Many of the people who had been listening walked back to the line.

Eric whispered, "That ghost sure made a lot of trouble."

Aunt Molly said, "I never liked ghosts."

Eric and Aunt Molly walked to their place in line. Cam didn't. She was still watching the old man.

The emergency medical people were holding the stretcher.

"I won't get on that," the old man said. "There's nothing wrong with me."

Cam looked at the old man. She blinked her eyes and said, *"Click."*

Rrrrrrr!

Sirens were blaring again. A police car drove up to the ticket booth. Two police officers got out of the car.

"Come on," Eric said to Cam. He was on his way to the ticket booth.

Cam didn't follow Eric. She watched the old man.

The young woman told the man, "You don't have to get on the stretcher. But you must come with us to the hospital. You need to let a doctor take a look at you."

"I'm not going to the hospital," the man said as he stood. "I don't need a doctor to poke at me and tell me what I already know. There's nothing wrong with me."

The man started to walk away. The young woman reached for his arm.

"Let me help you," she said.

"Leave me alone," the old man told her.

Then he walked toward the train station.

The emergency medical people watched the man leave. Then the young woman shook her head. She and the young man put the stretcher in the ambulance and drove off.

Cam walked to where the old man had been lying. Cam looked at the glasses, papers, and magazines the man had left behind. She closed her eyes and said, *"Click."*

Cam picked up the glasses. She looked through them and then put them in her pocket.

Eric ran to Cam.

"The police went to the train station. They're looking for the ghost," Eric said quickly.

Eric took a deep breath.

"With that costume on, he'll be easy to find," Eric said.

He took another deep breath.

"Eric," Cam said slowly. "He'll take off the

ghost costume. That was the plan. Then it will be very hard to find him."

Eric scratched his head and said, "You're right."

"If the police want to catch the thieves," Cam said, "they should come with me. I'll be looking for the old man."

Chapter Five

"The old man?" Eric asked. "Why are you following him? He didn't do anything."

Cam said, "I think he did. I think he and the ghost are partners. They're both thieves."

Cam was walking quickly toward the train station. Eric had to run to keep up.

Many people were leaving the train station. They all seemed to be in a hurry. Cam and Eric were going the other way. It was difficult for them to get through the crowd.

"The old man had a heart attack. He almost died," Eric said.

"No," Cam told him. "He pretended to have a heart attack. He wanted everyone to run to him. That way the guards wouldn't be near the ticket booth and couldn't stop the holdup."

Cam and Eric came to the train station entrance. A staircase led down into the station. It was a large and busy place. Cam was looking at the people below. She was trying to find the old man.

"Why do you think he's a thief?" Eric asked.

"Because he was wearing a disguise, too," Cam said. "That's why."

Cam took out the glasses.

"Someone who wears glasses doesn't forget them," Cam said. "But he forgot these. Look through them. They're just plain glass. They were part of his disguise."

"And the wig," Eric said. "Maybe that was part of his disguise, too."

Cam told Eric, "Look for someone wearing a bright yellow shirt."

"There he is," Eric said and pointed.

Cam started to run down the steps.

"Wait!" Eric yelled as he ran after Cam. "Wait for me!"

Cam stopped on the landing in the middle of the staircase. She held out her arm. Eric stopped, too.

"He's just standing there. He's looking for something," Cam said.

Eric leaned very close to Cam and whispered. "He may be dangerous. Shouldn't we tell Aunt Molly where we are?" Eric asked.

"Shh!" Cam said. "Look."

The old man went into a large coffee shop at the other end of the station.

"There must be bathrooms in there," Cam whispered. "He'll go in and take off his costume. Then we won't be able to identify him. Maybe the ghost is already in there."

Cam and Eric followed the old man into the coffee shop. They saw him enter a narrow hall on the other side of the shop. Above the hall was a restrooms sign.

Cam and Eric sat at a table.

"I'll wait here," Cam whispered. "When I see him leave the bathroom I'll know what he really looks like. You go get the police."

"Can I help you?" someone asked.

Cam looked up. A waiter was standing by the table.

"I'm not hungry," Cam told him.

"This is a restaurant, not a waiting room,"

the waiter said. He gave Cam and Eric menus. "I'll be back to take your orders."

Eric put his menu on the table and left the shop. Cam watched the hall leading to the bathroom.

The waiter returned to the table. "What would you like?" he asked.

"I'm waiting for someone," Cam said.

Just then Eric returned. The two police officers were with him.

"Over here," Cam called, and waved to them. "He went into the bathroom. He's taking off his costume. If you follow him, I'm sure he'll lead you to the ghost."

The police walked to the bathrooms. Cam and Eric followed them.

The police went into the men's room first. When they came out of the men's room one of the officers was carrying a white wig and a yellow shirt.

The officers knocked on the door of the women's room. When no one answered, they went in there, too.

Cam whispered to Eric, "Why are they going in there?"

The police came out of the women's room. One of the officers was holding the mask and white sheet the ghost had worn.

The officers looked around. Then they

pointed to an emergency exit at the other end of the narrow hallway.

"That's where they went," one of them said. And the two officers left through the emergency exit.

Chapter Six

"They took off their costumes. How will the police find them?" Eric asked.

Cam's eyes were closed. She said, *"Click."*

Cam said, *"Click,"* again.

"What are you looking at?" Eric asked.

"Click. Click.

"Do you have a pencil or pen? Do you have paper?" Cam asked with her eyes closed.

"I have a pen," Eric said. "I'll get paper."

Eric started to walk off. He quickly came back.

"Don't open your eyes," Eric said. "I'll be right back."

Eric went into the bathroom. He came out with a paper towel.

"The ghost is a woman," Cam said with her eyes closed. "We know that because the police found her costume in the women's bathroom. Now I'm looking at the pictures I have of her in my head.

"Write this down," she told Eric.

"She's not too tall and not too short. She's wearing white sneakers. She has long, thin fingers."

Eric wrote Cam's description on the paper towel.

"That's it?" Eric asked.

"I can tell you more about the man," Cam said. "He has brown hair, brown eyes, and bushy eyebrows. He has a small nose. And he's wearing black pants with cuffs."

Cam opened her eyes. She walked toward the emergency exit.

"Now we'll find them," she said.

"No, we won't," Eric told her. "We'll give your descriptions to the police. They'll find the thieves."

Cam and Eric walked through the exit.

"Oh, my! Thank goodness I found you."

It was Aunt Molly. She hugged Cam and Eric.

"I was standing in line," Aunt Molly said, "and I asked myself, 'Did I come here alone?'

TRACKS A-G →

"'No,' I answered myself.

"Then I remembered that you like to solve mysteries. I thought that maybe you followed the ghost into the train station. Thank goodness I found you."

Cam wasn't listening to her aunt. Cam was looking at the people in the train station. She was searching for the thieves.

"Look," Cam said. "There's a woman wearing white sneakers. And the man with her has brown hair. He's wearing black pants with cuffs."

Cam ran to the couple.

"Stop! Stop!" Aunt Molly shouted.

Some people in the station stopped. But Cam didn't. She kept running until she was standing near the couple.

Cam looked at them. They looked at her. Then Cam walked back to Eric and Aunt Molly.

"They weren't the thieves," Cam said. "The man didn't have bushy eyebrows."

"We didn't come here to catch thieves," Aunt Molly told them. "We came to buy concert tickets."

Aunt Molly pointed to the stairs and said, "Let's go uptown."

Aunt Molly shook her head. "Oh, my. I said that wrong. I meant to say let's go upstairs."

Cam, Eric, and Aunt Molly walked toward

the staircase. Cam kept looking for the thieves.

"There they are," Eric said. He pointed to the two police officers. "I'm giving them this paper towel."

"Why are you giving them a towel?" Aunt Molly asked. "Are their hands wet?"

Eric told Aunt Molly that on the towel were descriptions of the thieves. Then he showed it to the police officers.

"Thank you," one of the officers said. "But

I don't think this will be much help. We can't stop every woman we see wearing white sneakers."

Aunt Molly looked down and said, "I'm wearing white sneakers and I'm not a thief. I work for an airline."

"And I have brown hair and bushy eyebrows," the officer told Aunt Molly.

The other officer put the paper towel in his pocket. "My name is Officer Kent," he said. "My partner is Officer Feldman. Please call us if you remember anything else that might be helpful."

He wrote his name and the telephone number of the police station on his notepad. He gave the paper to Eric.

Cam's eyes were closed.

She said, *"Click."*

"Let's go," Aunt Molly said. "Let's get back in line."

Cam's eyes were still closed. Eric held her hand and led her to the staircase.

Eric whispered to Cam, "Take a step."

Cam stepped up. Then she said, *"Click,"* again.

"Take another step."

Cam took another step.

Cam said, *"Click,"* a few more times as Eric led her up the stairs.

"Now we have to find the man in the cloth business, the one wearing the suit," Aunt Molly said. "I asked him to save my place in line."

"That's it!" Cam said. She opened her eyes. "I know how to catch those thieves."

Chapter Seven

Cam told Eric, "I *click*ed and looked at the old man. When he first came out from the station he was holding papers and magazines."

"That may have been part of the plan," Eric said. "Those papers and magazines fell. Then it really seemed like the man was having a heart attack."

Cam said, "Many magazines are not sold at newsstands. They have a name and address on the cover. They are mailed to people at their homes."

Cam, Eric, and Aunt Molly were out of the train station. They were walking toward the line when the man in the suit saw them.

"There you are," he said. "I tried to save your place in line. But the line kept moving. Then it was my turn to buy tickets. I couldn't hold your place any longer."

Aunt Molly turned. She looked at the long line of people still waiting to buy tickets.

Cam whispered to Eric, "I have to find those magazines."

"Do we have to go to the end of the line?" Aunt Molly asked.

"Yes," the man said softly. "I'm sorry."

Aunt Molly took Cam's and Eric's hands.

"You have to stay with me. I don't want to lose you again."

Aunt Molly held on to Cam's and Eric's hands. She led them to the end of the line. As they walked, Cam looked for the magazines.

"*Ah!*"

Someone in line screamed.

"*Ah! Ah!*"

Other people screamed.

"I hope it's not another ghost," Aunt Molly said.

It wasn't. Triceratops Pops, the singing group, was walking toward the concert hall. And they were wearing their dinosaur costumes.

They waved. They stopped and spoke to

some of the people waiting in line. Some fans held out papers, and the Triceratops Pops singers signed them.

Fans ran from the line. They held out more papers and CDs to be signed. Soon a large crowd of people had gathered.

"Smile," someone shouted. "I'm taking your picture."

"Sing something," another fan called out.

"We have to go now," one of the singers said. "We have to rehearse. But we hope to see you all at the concert."

Cam, Eric, and Aunt Molly watched the T-Pops singers walk into the concert hall. The fans returned to their places in line.

Then Cam and Eric saw Officer Kent and Officer Feldman come out of the train station. The officers went to the ticket booth.

"I have to find something," Cam said to Aunt Molly.

"I don't want to lose you again," Aunt Molly told Cam.

"I lost a shoe in Tel Aviv," Aunt Molly said. "It was hard to walk with only one shoe. I don't like to lose things."

"I'm not a shoe," Cam said. "I just have to look for something. I'll be right back. I promise."

"Me, too," Eric said.

Cam and Eric went to where the old man had fallen. Eric found a sheet of lined paper. There was some writing on it. He gave it to Cam.

Cam looked at the paper.

"'Milk. Coffee. Orange juice. Toilet paper.' This is a shopping list." She put the paper in her pocket. "I'm keeping it as evidence."

Then Eric found two copies of *Picture News* magazine. He showed them to Cam.

Cam said, *"Click,"* and looked at a picture she had in her head.

"These are the ones the man dropped," Cam said, as she opened her eyes. "And look here." Cam pointed to a small white rectangle in the corner of one magazine. "Here's his name and address."

"Let me see that," Eric said.

Cam gave him the magazines. On the cover of each magazine was a label with the name "Mr. Peter Dowe," followed by an address.

"We just have to go to this address," Cam said, and pointed to the labels. "That's where we'll find the old man and the ghost."

Chapter Eight

"We're not going to a thief's house," Eric said. "That ghost has a gun! We're going to the police."

Cam and Eric went to the ticket booth. The police officers were there. They were talking with Sally. They asked her if she remembered anything else that might help them catch the thieves.

Officer Kent was very tall. Cam tugged on his sleeve and said, "I can help. This is the thief."

Cam gave Officer Kent one of the *Picture News* magazines.

Officer Kent and Officer Feldman looked at the magazine. A picture of the president of the United States was on the cover.

"You think the president dressed up as a ghost and stole the money!" Officer Kent said. "That's silly!"

Officer Feldman told Cam, "I saw him on the news this morning. He's in Washington."

"Not him," Cam said. She pointed to the white rectangle. "Him!"

Eric told the police officers about Cam's amazing memory. Then he told them about the old man, the shopping lists, and the magazines.

"Maybe these magazines were stolen," Officer Kent said.

Officer Feldman said, "And maybe they weren't. Maybe this thief left us his name and address. Let's find out."

Cam tugged on Officer Kent's sleeve again.

"Can we go along?" Cam asked.

Officer Kent looked at Officer Feldman.

"Maybe she can help us identify the thieves," Officer Feldman said.

Eric said, "Cam has an amazing memory. She's good at identifying people."

Cam and Eric walked with the police officers to their car. Officer Feldman opened the back door. Cam and Eric got in.

Officer Kent spoke into the car telephone. He told someone at the station where they were going. He asked that other police cars meet them there. Then he turned on the flashing lights.

Bam! Bam! Bam!

It was Aunt Molly. She was knocking on the windshield.

"Let them out! Let them out!" she yelled. "They're just innocent children!"

Cam said, "She's my aunt Molly."

Officer Kent opened the back door. "Get in," he told Aunt Molly.

"I'm innocent, too," Aunt Molly said. "I work for an airline."

Eric explained to Aunt Molly why they were riding with the police. Aunt Molly smiled and got in.

"I travel a lot," Aunt Molly said. "But this is the first time I'll be traveling in a police car."

Officer Feldman turned and said, "Put on your seat belts."

Officer Kent drove quickly. He went through red lights. People in other cars moved aside to let them pass.

As they sped through traffic, Cam and Eric smiled and waved to people they passed.

Officer Kent stopped the car in front of Peter Dowe's house. Police officers in three other police cars were already there.

"You wait here," Officer Feldman told Cam, Eric, and Aunt Molly. "These thieves might be dangerous."

Chapter Nine

Cam, Eric, and Aunt Molly watched the police surround the house. Officer Feldman knocked on the front door. Officer Kent and two other police officers were with him.

They waited.

Officer Feldman knocked again.

A man opened the door. Cam looked at him. She blinked her eyes and said, *"Click."*

The four police officers went into the house.

Cam closed her eyes and said, *"Click"* again.

"That's him," Cam said. Her eyes were still

closed. "He's the man I ran up to in the train station. He had bushy eyebrows when he pretended to have a heart attack, but not when I saw him later. Those eyebrows must have been part of the disguise."

Cam opened her eyes. She watched the police officers lead the man and woman out of the house. They led the couple to one of the other police cars.

Officers Kent and Feldman came back to their car.

"They confessed," Officer Feldman told Cam, Eric, and Aunt Molly. "They returned the money."

Officer Kent smiled. "Peter Dowe and his wife were surprised when we knocked on their door. 'How did you find us?' they asked. I told them we had the help of a smart young girl with an amazing memory."

"I helped, too," Eric said.

"Yes, you did," Officer Kent said.

Officer Kent drove Cam, Eric, and Aunt Molly back to the concert hall. The line outside the ticket booth was gone. In the window was a sign that said SOLD OUT.

"Oh, my," Aunt Molly said. "We won't get tickets to the Triceratops Pops concert."

"Oh, yes, you will," Officer Feldman said.

Officer Feldman knocked on the door to the concert hall. When the door was opened, he led Cam, Eric, and Aunt Molly inside.

The Triceratops Pops singers were on stage. They were rehearsing. Cam, Eric, and Aunt Molly sat in the front row and listened.

Officers Kent and Feldman spoke with Sally. Then she walked onto the stage. The music stopped. Sally spoke with Big Pop, the leader of the singing group.

Big Pop took a large envelope from his music stand. He came over to Cam and Eric. He took three autographed pictures of the band from the envelope. Then he took out three concert tickets.

"We save these for our friends," Big Pop said. He gave the pictures and tickets to Cam. "Thank you for catching the thieves."

"I helped," Eric told Big Pop.

The other band members and Sally all came off the stage to meet Cam, Eric, Aunt

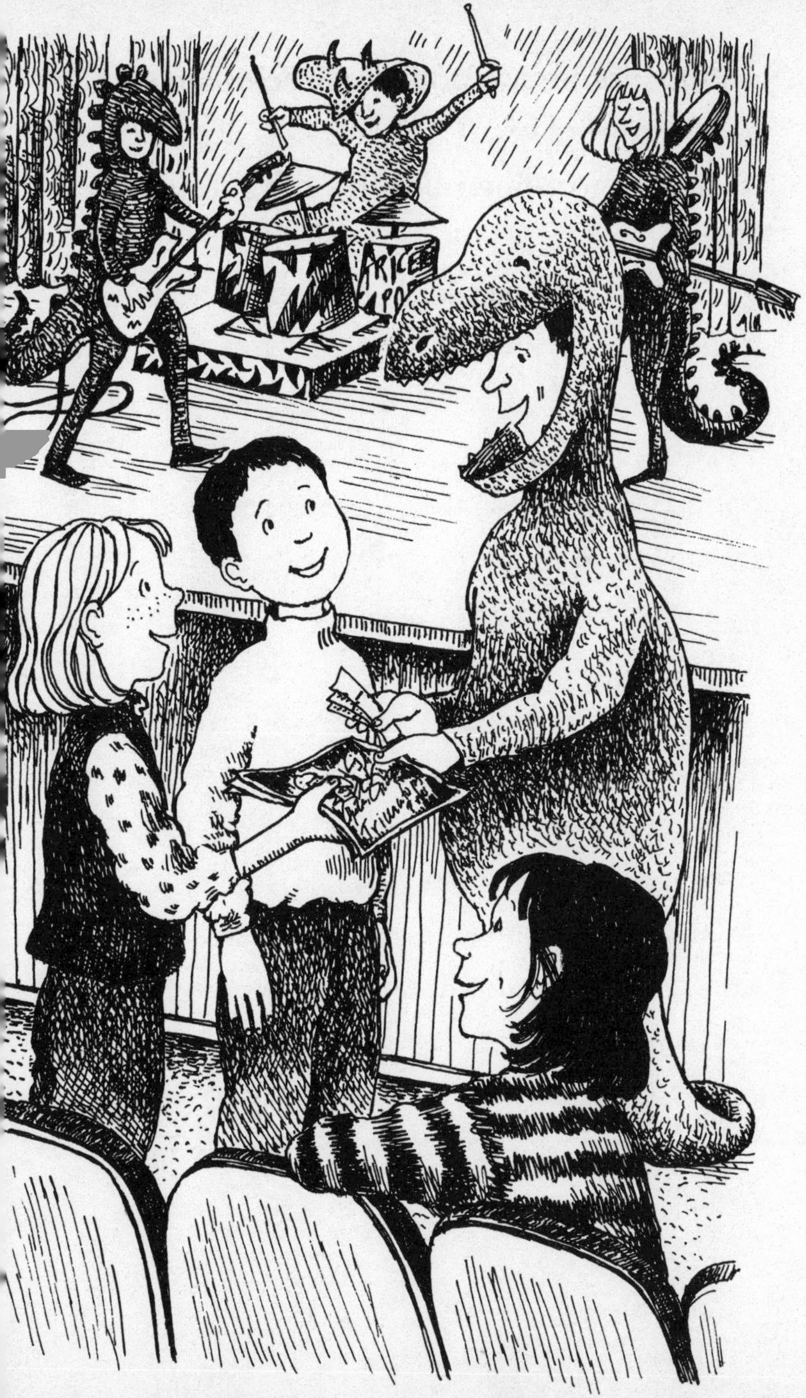

Molly, and the two police officers. Cam looked at everyone.

"I want to remember this for a long time," she said.

Then Cam blinked her eyes and said, *"Click!"*